THE NEW BIZARRO AUTHOR SERIES
PRESENTS

POLYMER

CALEB WILSON

ERASERHEAD PRESS
PORTLAND, OREGON

ERASERHEAD PRESS
P.O. BOX 10065
PORTLAND, OR 97296

www.eraserheadpress.com
facebook/eraserheadpress

ISBN: 978-1-62105-255-5
Copyright © 2018 by Caleb Wilson
Cover design copyright © 2018 Eraserhead Press

Printed in the USA.

Editor's Note

There are many kinds of heroes. Don't let anyone tell you that it ain't nothin' but a sandwich. Sometimes it seems silly to throw our respect and admiration behind some asshole with a guitar or some pretty face on the silver screen. What have they done for us? Caleb Wilson's Polymer presents the portrait of a man who is bigger than life, Ziggy Stardust and Professor Van Helsing rolled into one sword slinging walking can of whoopass. He's a curious character, Polymer and he's attracted a lot of love and attention. What does it mean to have that respect and adoration while having to be the person the crowd thinks you are? A rockumentary set ten feet outside of an 8-bit gothic fantasy, Polymer posits and plays with that question, while giving you some serious mind candy to chow down on during the show.

—Garrett Cook, editor

If we weren't behind this pane of glass we'd rush to him. The hunter formerly known as Liero. We hope that we're not just putting thoughts in his head when we tell ourselves that he must have found it liberating to have his face torn off. We were watching, a handful of the audience fainted when it happened, when the wretch's fingers dug into his ear, under his jaw, through his cheek, clenched, found their purchase, and ripped loose the skin that comprised all of his features. You should have heard us wailing. It seemed that he was going to perish from the sheer indignation of it, and the blood loss. His band saved him, faithful Captain Edgmond, Hictor and Mauve, and the doctors gave him a new face. Like all of us except for sociopaths or actors, Liero had always been slave to the expressions that moved the surface of his skin. With the new face came a new name and a new mystique that could not be betrayed by smiling or wincing.

Oh god, he's looking this way. A big cheer. His new

face is cyan neoprene, deadpan under slicked black hair. His jumpsuit, white satin. Cursive embroidery on the chest, magenta silk thread, spelling: Polymer. Around his neck on a plastic chain hangs a lucite cube with what looks like a shrunken head inside it. Those in the know are aware it is actually a tiny mutated potato that looks like a shrunken head. White gloves and white running shoes. Left leg bent, lunge extended by a rapier with a glass blade. Not glass, that's a common mistake, it's some translucent occult metal. He found it on a former run, deep in the Castle. A man who saw him find it starts telling the story: A reddish vapor twined up about a row of shattered columns...

On the other side of the glass is a hall of black and white linoleum. Muted echoes, poor light. The synthound evaded Polymer's lunge and is now circling back. Its gait is crooked and cowardly. We boo, screech our disdain. Its black claws scrabble at the floor. Rufous fur dangles in clumps, swings from flesh that is mange-marbled, pink and white. Always pointing at Polymer is the long lumpy snout. Just skewer it! We're jumpy tonight, don't want to see our idol slain in front of us. The synthound's single nostril blows a bubble of blood. The thing has no lips, no mouth. No eyes, just two shallow, furry pits. In a line down its belly are woofer nodules that thump a fuzzy life beat. The beat is hypnotic, its goal to confine Polymer's movements to the synthound's twitchy rhythm. Look at that, he's bobbing his head. A musicologist says, Look at that, he's got a few beats per minute advantage...

That's heresy, in a way, but you have to grab every advantage you can. We agree. We roar to show it. We'd let Polymer get away with anything if it meant him winning.

The synthound comes at him in a curve, tilted like a cornering motorcycle, springs. If it manages to wrap its lanky limbs around Polymer he'll never shake it off, it'll bind and hobble him, thumping deadening bass into him at point blank range before snapping his spine.

We're just about all of us holding our breath, grabbing the arms of those around us, pressed so close to the glass our breath blooms on it, Get down in front! Polymer leans back and the hound arcs past like a comet just missing a planet. Leaning back he thrusts his rapier forward, impaling the hound through the torso. A woman who sounds like she knows what she's talking about says, Just a jumble of organs and circuitry there. But he must have gotten lucky, punctured something vital, the thing thuds to the linoleum and curls up backwards into a hoop. Its life beat slows into a squall of static. There are about twenty of us in the audience, wedged in behind the glass, we jump up and down shouting his name, he must be able to hear us, he sends his cool plastic gaze at us... he nods his head. We go crazy.

Polymer twists the synthound's skull between his hands until something plastic inside its neck cracks and the flesh begins to pull apart. He rips the head loose, blood splashing onto his arms and chest, beading and flying off again to star the linoleum around his feet. His white shoes are speckled red. Someone points it out: They aren't liquid-repellent. You know, says someone else, I heard that's why he has twenty more pairs in boxes at home back in Sickleburg. It's the one piece of his outfit that doesn't last longer than a single run into the Castle.

What a star. From the pocket of his jumpsuit he takes

out a permanent marker. What a simple yet brilliant idea. Escaping the Castle now is no more complicated than following backwards the arrows he's drawn on the walls to mark his course through the maze-like halls. Linoleum underfoot, then flagstones, then bruise-colored marble, dead leaves, finely crumbled bricks. We follow along with him as best we can.

A bunch of us are there to greet him when he comes back into Sickleburg through the Laterine Vent. Hey, how are you feeling?

"Like I can relax."

You were amazing out there! Singlehandedly taking down a synthound, how did you...

"Thanks. Thank you so much."

There are just as many snares awaiting a hunter in the city as there are in the Castle beyond the vents that riddle the city. Polymer lets nothing touch him. Is that what we love about him? Look at that twinkling drop, on his face, that's not a tear, just the output of the artificial sweat gland installed by the surgeons.

What's next for you, Pol—

He's already off. We follow him. We have no shame, sorry to say!

The sky is all smeary clouds, the scales of a rotting fish. Here and there over the snaggle-toothed skyline shine weird lights from the vents. Polymer walks down between two rows of trees burnt to stubs and we hustle behind him at a respectful distance. A few of us try to scuttle up closer and we hiss shame at them to bring them back. Any one of us might approach, if we were alone, we wouldn't want to invade his privacy, but a mob like that: Hey! You! Get back here...

He steps over the junkies' feet that protrude

into his path. Right now the others are all slamming back drug-infused potions as well, in their armory. Captain Edgmond gets real freaky when he's under the influence. I think he's cute. Once I made out with Mauve and Hictor, says a little wisp of a man. Anyway, it's always more pleasant not to venture into the Castle unmedicated. The hunters will be laughing in wonder at the world. Smiling with the feeling that their lips are being lifted at the edges by fishhooks dangling from the ceiling. Everything grimy haloed with concentric rings of diamonds. We agree that it's best to replace the lacerations of teeth and razors with a gentle tickle. Of course all they're all just fooled by their own minds. Like these junkies we're treading on as we hurry behind our hero. All the drugs in Sickleburg are placebos.

Polymer turns a corner down a crooked lane. The grass is rank. At the end is a crowded plaza. We join in with them, these people standing in huddles, and now we're them and they're us. We're comparing rare potatoes with friends, and leaping aside as Polymer blazes a trail straight through us. Check it out, this potato is smiling like a saint. Hanging over the glass storefront is a sign, spiny black letters, Herkimer's Potato Showroom.

We all know about Herkimer. Polymer and Potato enthusiasts both. You have to know Herkimer. She's Polymer's friend, all right, probably his lover, definitely his lover. A woman opines: She has just the best luck, you heard about this, I'm not boring you, am, I? You heard this story? No, tell me. So she was managing this small potato shop at the exact time potatomania started. The owner of this place died without an heir meaning the city judges granted ownership to Herkimer without delay. Lucky too that the judges were too interested in smoking their placebo powder to linger over civil matters. Now she's one of the richest people in Sickleburg, will be until the potato bubble bursts.

We knew it: the potato showroom was Polymer's destination. In he goes and those of us stuck out here get just a glimpse of the interior. It's mostly dark, with white cones of light spearing down onto prized potatoes that lie on velvet platforms. Each potato is shaped like a different grotesque head. Bulging cheeks and brows, gaping mouths. Show potatoes, bred for expression, size, and the hard-to-define "surprise factor," command astronomical prices. A man says, I think they're a waste of money. Such an original opinion, someone shouts back, If you had any money you wouldn't think that! The place is packed, Sickleburgers desperate to experience some wonder, a bit of magical in the mundane. A few of us squeeze in after Polymer but most of us are stuck out here in the plaza.

We are burning up curious about what's going on in there. Polymer probably met Herkimer right away, maybe she was waiting for him, maybe he had to find her, eager to take her in his arms. No, no, someone says, that's not how it would be: their relationship is different, you know? We do know that: we've read the tabloids. Oh, the tabloids! There's got to be a reporter who can get in there and tell us what's going on, give us the private details that we know we deserve.

While we're waiting for that to happen, a bunch of us trade stories about Polymer. Two camps of us, not to get into too much detail, but there are those of us who have been following Polymer since he was Liero, and there are those newcomers who really became hooked once he had his new face. We old-timers like to tease the newcomers a little but really we're all on the same side. We all know how amazing Polymer is now. Just, those of us who knew him back before the injury, we have something special that, I'm sorry, the others just can't have.

A bunch of us were there, hard up on the glass, it was the whole band, and a wrinkled wretch jumped out at Liero, out of this electric coffin, and got its claws into the skin of his face. Captain Edgmond was pummeling some big shaggy brute and Mauve and Hictor were tag-teaming a withron in big clear armor, poor Liero was on his own. We could hear the flesh peeling away. It made a slurping sound, like a magnified kiss. Probably something like the sounds Polymer and Herkimer are making right now. You think they're loud in lovemaking? Oh no, I imagine them quiet yet firm, passionate statues. The wretch waved the scrap of skin like a flag. We shrieked. Edgmond executed the brute then came over and folded the wretch like a sweater. Little bits of its naked bones stuck out through the rags. Liero had been so sweet. Watching Polymer step out of the hospital six months later was like watching a butterfly hatch into a smooth, flawless caterpillar. We understand how he got a lot of new fans that day. And that was before he started dabbling in New Synth.

We love him for that. The authorities hate him. We're rebellious that way. Sickleburg's always had a big music scene, until fifty years ago when they invented New Synth. The sound and structure of it degraded the barriers between this world and another. It struck a chord with our grandparents' generation, New Synth bands grew up in basements like mushrooms. With every concert the synthesizers cut at the world like oscillating saws. Within six months unmendable cracks formed in Sickleburg's reality.

At first only the smells of the otherworld leaked through, mildew, rot, burning plastic, but then vents yawned open. You might come across a vent anywhere, in a garret, in a supermarket, in a broom closet or senate chamber, and see through the vent the rooms of a limitless Castle. The strains of New Synth spilled from it.

The authorities determined that the discovery of New Synth was no accident. It was a plot from beyond. The practitioners of New Synth were arrested, executed or de-fingered, though they were all dupes. Fiends came through the vents from the Castle every night and the people of Sickleburg got good at martial arts. Music was banned. Oh gods, a light, a candle, look there, the second floor. That's Herkimer's office/bedroom combo. They're probably having sex. Sorry, I can't, oh!

A little man in a tall hat is holding up a bale of something: a quickly printed tabloid. We snatch them up, ink still smeary, damp off the press, and start reading all about Herkimer and Polymer's tryst in her office/bedroom.

This has got to be made up. Doesn't it? There wasn't someone there, recording this, surely? We are so shameless. We'd read it anyway.

Polymer: "I'm doing it tomorrow." The author of the article describes how Herkimer is straddling Polymer.

Herkimer: "You're a fool to do it." Now Polymer is thrusting into her from behind. His white jumpsuit neatly folded on a chair beside the bed. This is so obviously fake. Why can't we stop reading it?

Polymer: "It's time." Herkimer rolls over, pulls Polymer on top of her.

Herkimer: "A few more orgasms then, before it's too late." Polymer twists around, so they form a sixty-nine.

Well, the candle has gone out, the moon is high in the sky, it doesn't look like Polymer is going anywhere tonight. We're all excited, from the fight with the synthound, from the article, from our imaginations, but the crowd is drifting apart. We divide into three parts, some of us go to the barracks to see if we can chat with the other hunters, some of us go the holy view to look at Polymer's family, and some diehards stay here, hoping maybe to see Polymer without his shirt on look out Herkimer's bedtime window in the middle of the night. We'll wait hours for just a glimpse of that chest.

Polymer and Herkimer have been having sex ever since he got out of the hospital after his face transplant. She doesn't seem to like him very much, that's just our opinion, but she's an important person now. We have this feeling that to some socially powerful people their lovers being "interesting" might be more important than liking them. Some us don't like her, but nobody can say that Herkimer's not important. It was a shock how quickly potatomania took the imagination of Sickleburg. The city's always been prone to fads and enthusiasms. Before potatomania, New Synth, before that, longs eras of vista worship and bloody feuds between almost identical agrarian cults.

That's where another group of us is headed, the holy view. It's where Polymer's family will be, that's where they always are. When we get there, climbing the tall staircase, edging out over nothingness, holding onto the vines, we can see their little alcove, flickering with firelight from a burn barrel. We don't usually try to talk to them any more, to them we're scum, and we think they're nuts, to be blunt. Still maybe one day we'll learn something about Polymer from watching his mother and father and sister. They're Watchers of the Vista. That's what they call it, make it sound a little more grand.

We can see their silhouettes around the barrel, passing the binoculars around. They're singing a hymn. The holy view looks just like any other view to all of us, and we have to think to Polymer too: otherwise why would he have left the fold? We can't really get in there with them, don't want to be pushed off the edge by a fanatic, but we think that all they are looking at, some ways down and across, unreachable, is a stretch of stone steps, curved inward, descending towards a dim and obscure space. There is a bit of sloped floor, a few indistinct blocks. Stone altars? Maybe. There are differing opinions, if not enough for a schism. Beyond the blocks is a square rim. At the holy hour, just before sunset, light pours down the steps and you can see it's a large space, and that something glitters at the back, like tinsel. Watchers of the Vista always get tongue-tied when asked to explain what's so special about the view. Nobody can figure out where the view physically is, maybe that's part of what makes it special.

Your son was amazing tonight! Barely a whisper, they probably didn't hear it over the hymn.

Over at the barracks we don't get any satisfaction either. The lower floor is all dark. What, a barracks with windows on the lower floor? Sure, it's a bit strange, it used to be a supermarket. Some of us scale the drainpipes to the upper floor, peep in to see what we can see, the hunters are all clustered together. A few of them in their underwear! A man says, Oh, they're pissed, I can tell. They're having a meeting. Steam coming out of their ears. Hmm? It's just an expression. You think Polymer showed them up today? It's not his fault he outshines them, shouts a tall woman. It's not his fault he's perfect.

A window up there slides open and a hunter's head sticks out. Go home, creeps! We love Polymer. Go home. Polymer! Polymer! Ought to go down and kick their asses... Who said that? Was it Edgmond? Some of us adore Captain Edgmond as well, though nobody as much as Polymer. The threat never materializes, anyway.

We disperse across Sickleburg. The day passes more quickly when we're not clumped together. We work in the factories, controlling the huge knitting machine like a giant spider surrounded by its own web, oh, who are we fooling, the knitting machine controls us. We are thieves, bums, library clerks. We dig potatoes in the fields. We dig up fewer and fewer regular eating potatoes. Some mutated potatoes with faces. Even more mutated potatoes that are on their way to having faces but haven't mutated in quite the right way yet. We all hope for a stunning strain, the next new face, but even then it'll be the bosses who get the credit. How sad that we, who break our backs over the shovels, are glad of the reflected glory from when the bosses' potato fields yield some valuable new potato face? It's no wonder that we're so interested in Polymer. He's the one who is destined to break us out of these ruts. What, you don't think we deserve that escape? What about even the chance of that escape?

When night comes we start to gather again. The

band of hunters are all planning a big run, they're going to go in through the Caprimulgus Vent. It's got a nice broad area outside the glass, we're all there waiting as night falls. We really love that moment when the balance of the light changes between us here in Sickleburg on the outside of the glass and the Castle hall beyond the vent. It's pinkish gray, then purple, then black out here, while inside it's dull red, then gleaming. The Caprimulgus Vent is home to a colony of whippoorwills, their questioning burble fills the air. Full dark out here now and the stage is set beyond the glass but there's nobody in sight yet, hunters or monsters. Some of us buy sausages from a vendor making the rounds, some feel our stomachs tighten with hunger, our faces twisting with jealously.

A woman screams in delight: Here we go! Two people are frolicking on the ragged red carpet beyond the glass, jesters. A little bit of a pre-show. They have a wretch's skull with the teeth removed, they caper back and forth, batting it to one another with their feet, ankles, knees. To use their hands seems a major faux pas. They get a good rhythm going, they can twirl around or do a backflip before clattering the skull back. LEDs twinkle from the skull's eye sockets, the thing still has a sinister life in it. But of course, what would be the point of the pre-show if it didn't offer a little taste of the hunters' cruel virtuosity we're here to witness?

Oh, hey, quiet down now, here come the hunters. The jesters blow away like dry leaves in the wind, and here they are. We scream, we clap, we stamp our feet. Those of us close to the glass pound on it! Is that safe? Don't worry, it's safety glass.

Captain Edgmond is looking very fine in a long black duster, black combat boots, and black tricornered hat. He wields a long mace, it takes incredible strength to swing that and smash a ribcage. The Edgmond devotees amongst us fling up our hands when he appears and tears run down our faces. We're imagining, we can't help it, that incredible strength throwing us onto a bed and letting us have our way with it.

Hictor is wearing a brocaded doublet tonight, he gets a few cheers out of us. A man mutters that he's trying too hard. He's right, Hictor's no Polymer. Hictor has an axe over his shoulder. The weapon is flashy, and not even very useful except in certain circumstances. Hictor wants to appear powerful, we think, and it's that desperate want that's the turn-off. Edgmond just is powerful without that neediness, and Polymer operates on a different plane.

Mauve has her fans too. She's deadly with daggers. She spins them, throws them, stabs with them. She's wearing a dark grey wrap, it looks a little like mummy bandages, and a cape. A woman says, Slash them into bits, Mauve! Mauve glances back, waves at us. Okay, we'll give her a cheer for that. We like all of them well enough, no matter how we grumble.

Here it is, though. We're not show business experts, except in the sense that actually we are, but here's the thing about these hunters, they do what hunters have always done, for the last fifty years, and we're tired of it. When Polymer comes in among them we go crazy, there's panting, weeping, tearing of clothing, some light swooning.

He's in his jumpsuit, clean shoes. Rapier at his side. Potato medallion, cyan face, black hair slicked back. He's not swollen with muscle and rage. He does have a perfect posture, he might as well have been posed with weights and counterweights. Since fifty years of hunter's expeditions haven't destroyed the threat from the Castle, maybe we just want to give a new type of hunter a chance? There are other reasons. A lot of us find Polymer really sexy.

Hey, we're getting distracted. Look, the hunters are having an argument. They're in a huddle. They're speaking quietly, we can hear them because the safety glass has patterns of holes in it at the edges. The sound of New Synth is swelling up from deeper in the Castle. It always does that before something bad happens. How does it know? We are definitely feeling some unease out here in the crowd.

Polymer is stepping away from the other hunters. Damn, what's he doing? Oh gods, he's doing it! He's going—he can't be going to—look, look, he's—Edgmond is pissed but doesn't want to be undignified enough to show it, especially with all of us watching, and Mauve and Hictor are trying to cheer him up. We can't quite make out what they're saying but it's probably something like, Let him go his own way, We can do what needs to be done here tonight, We don't need him, etc.

Look, Polymer is going over to that gap under the statue. We usually just ignore gaps like that in the Castle, the halls are full of them, where the walls spread apart irregularly, where the synth that carved out space in the world burred at the edges. Little spaces or holes that it seems like you might be able to fit through but there's nothing there. There's a prominent one just inside the Caprimulgus Vent, beneath the statue of some cube-headed demigod with male-pattern baldness and exorbitant muscles. A black crack, between the carpet and the edge of the wall. It's about a foot wide, stretches most of the wall along the hall. Polymer is walking towards the gap. A man faints. A woman says, That's it? That's where he's going? How will we see what happens next? We are overtaking by anxious babbling. Polymer climbs down into the gap. The last thing visible of him is his white glove. He's gone.

It really shakes our cohesion. A lot of us feel woozy, like we stood up too quickly, like we heard a piece of terrible news we weren't mentally prepared for. He's really gone, just like that? There are vents all across Sickleburg, places for us to watch almost any action the hunters care to get into, it's what drives our lives, but now Polymer's gone into a place with no vents.

We disperse. All feeling a little guilty that Edgmond, Hictor, and Mauve won't have an audience today, but sorry, we're really too shaken. We knew, some of us knew, because the tabloids said so, that Polymer was planning on going off on his own again, like he had when he fought the synthound, but this, we weren't ready for this. Maybe we didn't read enough tabloids. To the printing shops! As soon as there's any news, we want to be there.

We devour the rags as they come out. We read about what Polymer must be doing down below, we read about his battles, his narrow escapes. None of this really has the ring of truth to it, are we fools for lapping it up? We are desperate for any shred of news about our hero, maybe we can't be blamed for wanting to believe this nonsense.

Some of us follow the others. They are still in the Castle, doing the good work, slaughtering wretches, wrecks, synthetic beasts. They're skilled at it; surround and put down. It doesn't have that same magic, you know? They're grateful for the audience, but we can tell that they can tell we're disappointed not to be watching Polymer, and that's just a drag on the mood for everyone.

It's night, two days later, and have you heard this incredible thing? A new vent just opened up, an hour ago, it's down off the plaza by Herkimer's potato showroom. Workmen are installing glass now, it should be safe soon, ah, screw it, let's go now.

Vents don't open that often any more. When they do it's because some new seam of New Synth burst free. Sure enough, we can hear it now all across the plaza, those synths like dental drills, makes us all feel a bit soft inside, and a bit brittle too. Some of us are getting spontaneous bruises.

What can we see through this new vent. There's a

little section of tiled floor, a sharp slope down to the right. Down that way is a gleam of light, and that's where the pulse and hum of New Synth is. There's a gasp, then a hush, Polymer just walked into the light. He came from above, from the left, and he's headed down into the light. We clap hard enough to rupture our palms. Desperate whistles, tears.

He still has that perfect grace, but Polymer's a little the worse for wear. Oh, gods, don't even suggest such a thing! Any little flaws around the edges only make him better, really. His shoes are filthier than ever, his hair is mussed, there are little holes all across the front of his jumpsuit, stains that the fabric couldn't resist. There is, maybe, the smallest, just the tiniest suggestion of a limp. Could be a swagger. His hair is mussed but that's all right. A lot us, we find that we like it better. His rapier is covered with blood and oil. He has two medallions now. There's Herkimer's memento, the tiny potato in lucite, and something else; a piece of electronic gear, it looks like, on a thick plastic cord. It's got buttons, blue and green lights, some kind of touchpad facing out from the center of his chest.

We shriek, and Polymer hears us through the glass, looks up wearily. We raise the roof. We're actually outside but you get the idea. A woman shouts, Polymer, what happened? Where were you? What's going on?

He waves, slowly. He face is deadpan. We can usually read so much into that blank face, anything we want, really. For the first time ever, it's hard. What has happened? We have no way of knowing. We can conjecture a fierce battle. Battles, maybe. And what's going to happen next? We have no idea. We're in new territory here.

Polymer walks down the slope to the right, and straight out of view of the vent. We gasp again, then groan, you're killing us here. Just a few of us can still see him, and this is amazing: He's touching the electronic pad on his chest, he's moving his fingers, tapping and twirling them. Even those of us who can't see can hear a twining sawblade of sound, a synth as pure and cutting as anything that came from the Castle. Everyone gathered in the plaza sees the vent widen downward, the cobblestones and the dirt underneath them peeling apart, the rent widening into the air, and bringing Polymer back into view again. He's now at the lowest extent of a long, crooked hole between Sickleburg and the Castle, and the lower part has no safety glass. This is thrilling, we haven't felt anything like this in years.

We rush up to the edge, reaching over, we're almost within touching distance of Polymer, he could do it, he could come over and meet us, but we wouldn't want to distract him. We clamor for his attention anyway. The New Synth is loud enough without the glass to cause nosebleeds, mild hemorrhaging. Give us back some of the adoration we're giving you! Polymer glances our way, his face a rubbery nothing, we go dizzy with screams. He strokes the touchpad at his chest, then a triple tap, and a synthsaw cuts another long jagged streak down to the right.

The architecture of the plaza is sagging now, a long drooping causeway that runs along the vent, and we plunge along it. It takes a moment to hit us. We're in the Castle! Polymer is bringing us new places. This is the kind of thing that makes us love him.

Polymer descends a hallway lined with pottery urns. One is partly smashed, a skeletal leg dangling out. We figure each one for a vessel of execution, simple yet horrid. At the far end of the hall a wretch drifts down from the ceiling, red rags fluttering around it like it's drifting underwater instead of through the air. We groan in despair, but we should have faith, this is a different hunter now than the Liero who lost his face to such a monster. Under the floating rags the wretch is all bones and negative space. Warped and yellowed bones repaired, where they have split, with electrical tape. Joints strengthened with rusty wire. Dangling from a finger, a grip so loose that it must be supernatural, and impossible to break, even for Polymer, is a sword with a wide triangular blade, it pulses a syncopated rhythm in waves of violet radiation.

Look out!

Polymer whirls around, lifting his rapier, and barely manages to deflect a blow from the second wide triangular blade. Purple sparks fly out from where the swords crossed. Wretches always travel in pairs. The second one drifts sideways through the air and just out of reach of Polymer's returned thrust. Under the tattered red cowl its skull wobbles and bobs like an amateur's marionette. We think this is the wretches' approximation of laughter.

Polymer approximates laughter too. His is silent and it does not move his face. A pair of red wretches like this should bring about the quick slaughter of a single hunter. They think they have him. Our hearts are beating so fast our chests feel like jelly. We don't even register what horrible peril we are in ourselves.

The wretch's sword flashes at Polymer's eyes. The synth node installed between its teeth whistles hypnotically. We all go a little mad. Polymer throws up his hands. He sags. His rapier falls, bounces on the stone floor. When the wretch settles down over him, gentle as a jellyfish, Polymer surges up, inside the reach of the sword, and laces his fingers through its ribcage. He's tapping at the device on his chest, a rhythm to counteract that whistle. The whistling falters and stutters. Bones splinter as he rips the wretch's carcass apart like kindling. The synthetic whistle dies in a crackling arpeggio.

This is the best moment of our lives. We are surrounded by the stink and glory of occult combat, deep in the Castle. We are filled to the eyes with adrenaline.

Polymer takes up the weapons and races toward the second wretch. When he reaches the end of the hall it hovers near the ceiling and far out of reach. He flings its companion's sword, a purple-sparking arc. The sword misses. The thing whistles forlornly. Polymer plays a blast of synths and opens his and our craggy path. We move on.

The hallway spits downward, narrowing into a brutalist wedge. At the bottom is an archway, a blaze of red light through it. Some of us are looking back now, a winding, ragged path, a crack through shale now, with the air of Sickleburg somewhere, how far back? We are exhilarated. Even though it stinks down here, like carrion. We think that we can probably get out of here if something goes wrong. Most of us, at that moment, deep in a kind of rapture, don't even care.

In front of the archway stands a withron, encased in its transparent suit of armor. The armor is translucent metal, the same material as Polymer's sword, maybe. It hulks about eight feet high, stout legs with pointed boots, a conical helm, arms like tree trunks. A long-handled maul stands beside it, balanced on its black metal head, which has the prongs and protrusions of an anvil.

A bunch of us all start screaming at the same time, Smash it, Polymer! Tackle it! Crack that armor, synthscore it! Polymer looks around, some of us hush, a little embarrassed, like the sun or the moon itself just noticed us, but others don't even care about that either. Wooooooooeeeeeyeah.

The withron itself is a bundle of wet and moldy skin, like the twist of matted netting that requires a plumber to fish from a bath drain. Scummy eyes stare from its mildewed face, which leans against the inside of the armor, leaving spore-smears as it adjusts its position. It moves its wasted arm and the corresponding arm of the armor reaches down and grasps the maul's handle, lifting it as easily as a tennis racket. Its other arm, twig-thin and sloughed around with skin like an oversized sleeve, lifts as well, and inside the clear armor, the tiny fingers begin to snap in beat.

Polymer tries to start a synth beating in opposition, but if the snapping fingers are hurting him like they're hurting us then our hero is in serious trouble. Each snap is like a nail sunk into our skulls. Our brains are feeling sizzled, like in that old breakfast food poster campaign, This is your egg, scrambled. The withron's beat is too plain, too primal to be subverted.

We feel all our hearts beating now in the same rhythm. Polymer staggers. We are falling to our knees, wiping away the tears springing to our eyes. The withron knight dances forward two steps, back one step. Two steps forward, one step back. Polymer stands rooted, seemingly all he can do is bob his head in time to its snapping fingers.

The suit of armor reaches him and steps back and forth for a space of eight measures, then raises its maul for a killing blow.

We are out of our minds with fear and, we should really admit this, a little delight. This is what we're here for, isn't it? It wouldn't be as life-changing if there weren't that special stink of despair.

We know Polymer slips away every night to practice his music. He's so secretive, up there in his cork-lined room. But will it help him get out of this?

Right on the beat the maul comes smashing down. Polymer's body knows what to do, his legs and feet go smoothly into motion. He moonwalks backwards and the maul misses him by an inch.

With a single beat in which to work, and hard against the knight's armor, he lifts the point of his rapier to a crack at its waist, shoves it through. Metal squeals on metal, and the blade slide in and pins the withron through its moistly sagging face.

We are silent, then volcanically happy. A man shouts, Yeaawh, yeaawh, YEAAWH. We experience some blubbering. We are hugging each other, kissing each other, we are a glowing knot of comrades all basking in Polymer's shared success.

Polymer draws the rapier back out. The armor collapses with a clatter while the withron writhes like a chopped worm. What were we even worried about? So smooth. Polymer glances over as us, tips his rapier up, and as one we salute him. He strokes the touchpad and the vent widens. The New Synth surges loud enough that our hair starts to fall out and our fingernails start to shake loose. Our teeth, like the walls of Sickleburg, start to grow new cavities.

We will never forget this. Of course, we aren't all down here to see this amazing show, some of us had other duties that couldn't be avoided, jobs, children, court dates, the kinds of things that didn't matter at all compared to the chance we lost out on, but how could we know at the time? We'll kick ourselves later, when the others come back, but at the moment, we're not finding the afternoon so terrible. While our comrades are deep down a jagged vent, going where no citizens of Sickleburg have ever ventured, the others of us stuck above are passing around the newest tabloid. There's a new article in here, it's really something: a Polymer enthusiast has written something special. He claims that this is all true, from a primary source, we have to say this has the ring of truth to it. So according to this article, here's what happened to Polymer after he climbed down that vent two days ago and left Edgmond, Mauve, and Hictor.

*W*hat happened during Polymer's lost forty-eight hours? Always remember, you read it here first. The answer has been revealed to your humble correspondent through crystal peering most intensive, indeed, some might even say excessive. Have you ever stared at something so hard and with such yearning that your eyeballs started to see squiggling lines floating everywhere? Floaters, they call them. But my dears, I know you're not reading this for my ophthalmological insights. You just want to know what I saw in my crystal ball. Read on, then.

I saw Polymer climbing down into the black crack. Nimble as a spider monkey, or a monkey spider. He fought horrors, a cackling little creep with eyes rimmed by dark and glossy feathers, and this vile lackey tried to betray Polymer, but got himself shanked first. I watched him tangle with a cube-headed mystic all covered with lambswool. He had the widest and most beautiful diamond-paned eyes. He talked in a lilting flood, I could see his chapped lips pinching and pursing as he yammered, *and he didn't have teeth but a row of little yellow bird beaks. His beaky mouth twittered sweet illusions and all the while he was slowly and lovingly pressing a stiletto through Polymer's temple. Our hero didn't feel a thing until the needle blade pricked bone, then some string of civilization snapped within him like it had been tuned too sharp and he went berserk, ripped off patches of the mystic's woolly skin, tore the thing apart like a dog ravaging a teddy bear. Avert your eyes, those of you with weaker stomach: it was a teddy bear filled with pearly pinkish fluid, like a mixture of blood and cake frosting. It never stopped smiling or whispering sugary lies until he tore its cubical head into two irregular polyhedra.*

I was watching when Polymer found the studio. He came in through a hole in the ceiling, down through the drop ceiling. Foamy hexagons all up the outer walls like scale, inner walls of glass, banks of burnished instruments, and burnt orange shag carpeting. They use it for reasons of damping the echoes, my dears.

I can report that Polymer wandered that strange place through an almost religious gleam. He was bent and stained from his ordeals, I know this is painful to read of. He was bent, but not broken. I saw him run his fingers over the ranks of machinery, over keys and switches and pumps. I saw him shake with some kind of laughter-haunted despair. Polymer's practice routines are well-known, he had planned on finding something simple, some instrument that anyone could pick up and quickly master. It was assumed that anyone could be a synth virtuoso. Its timbre that of something that had always existed and would outlast humanity, like the soulless shimmer of starlight. Could synth be hard to learn? Yet Polymer was riddled with doubt. I know that some of you must hate me at this moment. I say again, Polymer was riddled like wormy fruit, but what's a hero if not that rare person who never freezes, even when rotten to the core with doubt?

I was witness when Polymer found the portable synthesizer. Such a simple device. Foolproof. And for not-fools? A true omnitool. It was designed to be worn around your neck on a cord. It had a few switches and knobs along the top to alter the sound, and a square touchpad on the front to control it. Polymer slung it around his neck and poised his fingers over the pad. You won't believe what I saw next. HS.

This part becomes instantly famous, becomes a mummery, sooner than you'd think possible we're watching reenactments of it all across Sickleburg: an impersonator playing the part of Polymer, white jumpsuit looking authentic from a distance, face covered with a blue mask, he has the body language down pretty well. He's on a little stage thrown up within the boles of mossy trees or behind a closet door or between the potato hills in a rooftop garden. While Polymer is below we'll do anything to indulge ourselves.

Prop portable synthesizers dangle from our Polymers' chests and there are always three vocalists standing in the wings to voice the synth. Bass, Treble, and Midrange to give it that biting hum. If the police come, deniability: No officers, sorry for the confusion, there are no synths here, we're just actors! In from the other side of the stage always a little before the audience is prepared for it lurches Shhoggafrog.

We scream a little, muffle our mouths, giggle behind our hands. Shhoggafrog, the monster we love to hate. We write fan fiction about Shhoggafrog. We argue about how to pronounce his name. We love to hate Shhoggafrog so much that some of us have started to actually love him. It: we should really say IT when we refer to this sexless, ageless, impossible, unknowable elder thing. It is sort of cute in a grotesque way.

Our humble correspondent once wrote: *Shhoggafrog rippled forward on a ridge of rugose flesh, whorled black and white and lubricated with strings of clotted ichor, and clusters of hollow quills quivered there along its ghastly prow, fulfilling the purpose of fangs or fingers, or some other purpose more alien. Above the wall of foetid footflesh drooped huge weak wings covered with feathers of a greasy ebon sheen. As the flabby yet horrendously muscular body surged forward the quills rattled and the feathers shook like the hideous ritual appurtenances of some depraved and decadent religious order.*

Our mummery Shhoggafrogs are a little more homespun, but we still get a kick out them. You need three people inside a Shhoggafrog costume otherwise it's hard to capture the feel of the alien wriggling. One person arches over backwards, moves crabwise upside down, and another person crawls feet first under the arched person, and another person is draped on their stomach over the feet-first crawler. They're all festooned with dusty feathers and black and white cloth to form Shhoggafrog's hideous piebald integument. It takes a bit of practice but the three mummers can get a good kind of funky arrhythmic pace going and make their Shhoggafrog genuinely menacing as it surges across the stage towards the Polymer.

They have a battle. Polymer's wooden sword rings on the tambourine jingles hidden beneath the Shhoggafrog's feathers, he leaps in and out of combat, we cheer every strike and boo hiss when Shhoggafrog rears up to flail its wings at him. The actors tease us for a while, they don't have a set way of performing it, they like to read the crowd and can spin it out, but at a certain point Shhoggafrog makes its final lunge and wraps Polymer up in its wrinkled, greasy folds. Dozens of quills pierce Polymer's chest. The quills pulse and shake, sucking his blood out through the hollow centers and now we have a better idea of their function: drinking straws.

He twitches, he writhes, he twerks though with deniability, and then he strokes the touchpad. The vocalists start their buzzing three-part harmony and stagehands lace the air with laser pointers. The feathery cloak of Shhoggafrog is ripped up and away, riding on a wire, and the actors inside are shown now to be dressed in skintight pink and gray bodysuits. Now they are spilled organs, rolling and wrestling one another as red blades of synth slice Shhoggafrog to ribbons.

We clap and whistle. It's always fun, but just not quite the same as the experience of those lucky ones who are way down the vent, close enough to Polymer to see the false tear of his sweat glitter on his cyan cheek. To smell the decay of the Castle.

To us, the lucky ones, the rest are just hugging a simulacrum with all their strength. We wouldn't want to say it's pathetic, but we do pity them, just a little.

These lucky ones of us, we're watching as the real Polymer strokes his synthesizer, extends the ragged route down past the withron knight. Sickleburg is too far above us to see, to smell. We are humming with pride and full of nerves. We're right there with him, at his side as we descend into levels of the Castle we've never before imagined.

Polymer moves toward a rancid light ahead, open air. He leaves us behind, we're on a ledge with a chasm between us, he drops down a short distance into, all right, not open air, but a huge room, into which he has sheared a new entrance. The room seethes with activity around a dais, a glass throne with golden cushions. He absorbs the shock with his knees, is glancing around and gathering his wits when four withron sentinels dash at him from each direction. Their clear armor is more slender than the knight's and they move as quickly and unpredictably as cracks across glass. A woman cries out, Behind you! One clubs him in the kidney, one in the side of the head. One snatches his rapier and the other sweeps his leg, bringing him to the floor, and all four of them pile on. All we can see are his hands flailing at the shag carpet and then they fall still.

We're stuck to the view, like there are nails in our eyes. The withrons are dragging Polymer across the expanse of shag. His feet produce twin furrows through the bloodred fibers. The pulse of New Synth is painfully present. We're hallucinating, flashes of cubes, glowing pyramids, spheres stacked on spheres.

The room is vast, buttresses flying at weird angles everywhere we look. Crowded too, withrons of all shapes and sizes, courtiers scuttling back and forth. The sentinels haul Polymer towards a person who we instantly can see is the center of power in the room, or the absence around which a whirlpool spirals. He's facing away from us, a man of medium height, white blousy shirt, curly black hair tied into a pigtail with a red ribbon, tight black pants, pointy black shoes with rather high heels. His right arm is on his waist, and in his left he holds something up as if for inspection. It's on the other side of him, so we can't see it clearly, something long and floppy, a coat-like garment, maybe.

This man cocks his head toward Polymer and we shudder to see that he has no face. Then he turns a little more and we see that he does have a face, with exceedingly uniform features.

"Who's this?" The man's voice is smooth as wet silk, and when he speaks the illusion of his perfect face is cracked. We can see our mistake now, understand our confusion. His face is perfectly formed, and yet it is perfectly wrong: the inverse of a human face, a concave bowl into his head beneath his shining, curling locks. When he looks directly at us all is well. At an angle, or when he speaks, worms of disgust crawl through us.

One of the intruders, says a withron.

The man stares at Polymer. His voice is quiet, yet cutting as a scalpel, you could hear him whisper in a raging mob. "Welcome. Impressive of you to have made it so far. I am Lord Abisma, and it is my domain into which you are interloper." Exotic synths crackle and hum off him like liberally applied cologne. We're finding ourselves short of breath. Polymer must be too. He's twisting around in the hands of the withrons but they seem to be locked tight, he'd need a crowbar to break that grip, and every time he tries to twitch in rhythm their hands jerk him off balance.

"I will destroy you," says Polymer. We cheer half-heartedly, but it's hard to feel optimism, right now.

The other does not react. Abisma turns slightly and we can see what he's holding; a desiccated corpse, shrunken and dried like it has spent five hundred years in a desert tomb. But the clothing it's wearing, a tailed tuxedo in the style of Sickleburg, is fresh, we have the horrible realization that the corpse is that of a man who minutes before was one of us. He traveled down the slanted way with us, until he was snatched by Abisma's power, and none of us noticed it happen. It's quite a blow to our morale. We can hear the mutters going through the crowd, as we realize what happened. A man says, Is that... Jon? A woman answers, He was standing right beside me, someone else, When did it happen, and another one says it out loud but we're all thinking almost exactly the same thing, That could have been me down there, shriveled up like last year's roadkill.

Abisma hands the body, seemingly hardly heavier now than its coat and pants, to one of his servants, he steeples his hands below the perfect concavity of his face. He turns to another of his servants, one of dozens scuttling like foosball players up and down the room, and our stomachs turn sideways at the sight of his face.

We raise a muted whoop at the sight of Polymer, stoic.

Abisma's earworm whisper: "We've been monitoring the rest of them, yes?"

Yes, master, says the servant. Two men and a woman. They have been enjoying their usual success in the outer layers.

"I see," says Abisma. "Clearly we have been involved in an underestimation. I hate that. Why don't you bring them in and then we'll question them."

And this one? asks the servant, gesturing to Polymer like he is a garment hanging in a closet. Is the master still hungry?

"No, thank you," says Abisma. "I do want to talk to him, but later. I'm busy now. The most wondrous melody just came into my head and I wish to explore it for a while in my studio." He spares Polymer a brief, dead glance. "Lock him up."

Yes, master.

"Wait a moment." Abisma grins cavernously. He points a perfectly manicured finger at Polymer's chest. "You find it tasteful to wear two medallions? How gauche." Then Abisma leans forward, as if seeing for the first time the exact nature of the lucite potato medallion around Polymer's neck. His grin turns bleak. His nose a nose-shaped divot, his full lips runnels carved into perfect skin. "No, I take it back. You can't understand how happy it makes me to see you wearing such a thing."

"What, this?" Polymer tries to lift his arm, the withrons prevent him, and Abisma scolds them.

"Let him; we're in no danger here."

Polymer takes the potato medallion in his hand, jerks it down. The plastic chain snaps, and he tosses the potato to Abisma's feet.

"It's a symbol of your vanity and stupidity both, you see," says Abisma. "Of all of you. I invented the mutagen that will soon destroy your city's main source of food, yet I never would have imagined that you would be such willing collaborators in your own fate."

Polymer scrabbles at the synthpad still hanging on his chest. "Who's vain and stupid? Collaborate with this, motherfucker." He stabs down with his finger. All our hearts are flying up, we're surging up on wings of hope we didn't know we still had the mental strength to unfurl, and beams of white and magenta synth skewer out from Polymer in all directions. Abisma leans back like a sapling in a high wind.

Polymer swirls his finger on the pad and the synths line up, cohere into the proper rhythm. The bloody shag gapes under Polymer's feet, a tired and slumping abyss yawning open, he stands there on the edge for a moment, and then drops out of sight.

His rapier is still lying there on the carpet. We are in shock, but, maybe, the good kind? We scream so loudly that it's hard to say whether our voices or ears have given out first. We have forgotten to clap. A few of us raise our hands as if in worship. We are noticed. Lord Abisma turns his head, flies toward us, is suddenly among us.

We panic, some stumbling deeper into the vent, falling over the raw edges, we call out as we fall, until our breath runs out, some of us tumble down into the throne room where the withrons' transparent fists quickly pummel us into jelly, ribcages not up to the job of protecting our organs from this trauma, blood sheathes clear metal, seeps and laps down into the already-red shag, skulls fragment, limbs snap and twist and warp. Is this how the twisted frames of wretches are formed? Others of us run, searching with the mindless surging thrust of a mob or amoeba for the way back up, to the light and the relative safety of Sickleburg.

Glancing back, it is clear to all of us who escape that Lord Abisma is letting us go. He could have destroyed every one of us without effort. There he stands, as we flee, looming between a man and woman, his arms around the shoulders of both of them. Many of us know them, Marc and Shelley. They're not a couple, just had the back luck to be standing beside one another. Their faces warped with terror, shining with tears. Abisma's hollow face also warped, with a predatory smile. Good bye, friends, we are painfully sorry.

Polymer throwing down that potato medallion is both the end of an era and the start of the next. It is the end of Potatomania, the start of Polymermania. Those of us who watched Polymer's confrontation with Lord Abisma, those of us who made it back up to daylight, it was about two thirds of us, are the real catalysts behind that change. It wasn't anything, he probably didn't mean anything by it, but everything down there under the city was heightened, everything granted extreme meaningfulness, at least it did in our retelling.

Of all the potato dealers, it's Herkimer who stays solvent. We consider it her good luck coming through once again. Fortunes are ruined, rich people disgraced, whole piles of vegetables worth a million dollars one day rotting to slime the next, but Herkimer just turns around and starts selling sex tapes of her and Polymer.

Many of us buy the tapes. Sure it feels wrong but that's part of the thrill. They're grainy and off-kilter, like the frame rate has been changed. We've all been fooled, it's not what we really want, though only some of us realize it. Some things you just can't capture on videotape. Still, the placebo effect is strong.

There's a sense of the apocalypse around Sickleburg. Foundations are undermined, buildings collapsing, the sound of New Synth which had been quieted for decades now grows louder every night. For all that we are yearning for any glimpse of Polymer, now more than ever, he is proving elusive. We keep hearing rumors about new vents splitting open, just narrow cracks, they stretch far into the depths of the otherworld. You can hardly fit a fingertip through but can somehow see deep inside. A natural camera obscura maybe.

We like to imagine that these windows are the results of Polymer's synths, wherever he is. We stand in clumps around them, and once or twice a day one of us will see a flash of white jumpsuit, seemingly miles away, or a flash of cyan neoprene, an arm windmilling around to direct the synths. Some of us lose our jobs. Too tardy, too many or too deadly accidents at the mills. We'll survive. Others are plenty willing to share food and umbrellas.

A few of us maintain old interests, watch the bigger glass-fronted vents for the other hunters. This evening, through the Calverian Vent, crammed with broken skulls, a dozen of us are watching when Captain Edgmond, Mauve, and Hictor are waylaid by a team of eight withron commandos. The commandos wield batons and catchpoles with nooses of coated cable.

What a weird mix of emotions running through us as we watch the tragedy. A few of us, on what we think are heavy drugs, attribute to self-medication the deadness of our souls. There's sadness, the kind that's almost happy, because once the worst happens you don't have to be worried any longer about what will happen when the worst happens. And also some scorn at these so-called heroes, who might not be all about to die if they hadn't alienated the one true hero among them. We are not under the impression that there is any way these three hunters will survive.

For a few minutes they defy our expectations. As the commandos dodge and roll, trying to maneuver behind the hunters, Mauve plants a dagger through a moldy face, and Hictor knocks the head of one clean off with his axe. A stench, rotten beyond rotten, seeps through the air. Edgmond is a whirling fury. Then four more withrons converge from the shadowy skull piles. Edgmond goes down under a heap. Nooses arc down across the hall and slip tight over the hunters' necks. The lights in that wing of the Castle go out. The flat sounds of the termination of combat continue. A chill comes over us, like someone walking over our proverbial graves, and we find that we all have other places we need to be just now.

Several of us have the idea to try to connect again with Polymer's family on their turret. The idea arises organically, at a coffee shop, one of the places where we used to gather after seeing Polymer, when it was common for him to be seen. Now it just serves hot water, but the place still smells faintly of the precious roast.

We are all staring into our chipped mugs when a woman says suddenly, What about the holy view?

His family? They spend their whole lives looking, we want to look and see... A man says, Yes, it seems like we could learn something from them... Maybe even teach something to them... Most of us drift away at this point, back to our sex tapes and sugar pills. But this hungrier core, this needier core, we are committed to doing whatever it takes to find our Polymer. We'll go so far as worshipping the view for a time, maybe we'll find that there's something to their practice after all.

Creeping past the vines, we find the devotees more welcoming than we expected, they make us wear blindfolds for the first few days, feed us on sugar water, we have to be in the right mental state when we are first allowed to see the holy vista. We were right to come here. Already we are glad we shed our old companions like the fools they are. You had too little faith. We will never share what we see here.

For the rest of us, there are always the tabloids: *Dear readers, for some time now I have suspected that your humble correspondent cannot possibly be alone in wondering what the Vista Worshippers gather from their ceaseless vigil. I was not among those welcomed with blindfold and potion to share in their ritual, but of course, as you well know, I have other means of investigation at my service.*

The light of my fireplace reduced to that which pulses behind the cracks at hearts of embers, I peeped into my crystal ball, point of view roving to that abandoned neighborhood in the northeast of Sickleburg, up the moss-rotten steps, out along the holy ledge to the holy turret, there to move amongst the practitioners of that high and private sect.

I saw the erstwhile Liero's mother, Agat Estoc, a high priest of the Vista Worshippers. I admired her denim cloak and broad tinfoil headpiece. His father, Zeero Estoc, scholar of the ineffable, wore a mask that was a small replica of himself, which also wore a mask that was a small replica of itself. And so on. Presumably all of his masks wore masks down to infinity, though I choose not to burn out my crystal ball in so confirming. His sister, Ether Estoc, a mystical Knight of the Prospect, dressed in clattering scale armor made of flattened tin cans, though she quickly, by some unknown sense, detected my observation of her, her face twisting into a scowl that anticipated delight in carnage.

I rapidly steered away my point of view lest I discover she also had some method of gripping my throat across the astral plane.

At the edge of the turret was the narrow spot from which the holy view itself is visible. These famous places, visited in person, are always smaller than one expects, and I suppose the same is true for gazing on them through crystal. On this edge stayed, for twenty-three hours of the day, ancient Goerges, the oldest of the View Worshippers. It was Goerges who told the new arrivals what they might expect to see when they first began their observations.

There is a spotlight, which comes on as if in anticipation of the entry of some entity. The entity has not thus far ever arrived. There is a stone block. The block is thought to be either a chair or a low table. Either way it is considered to be inessential to the religion. There is the black-painted rim of wood. This is a stage. It is supposed by many that when the entity implied by the periodic shining of the spotlight does enter, it will be onto this stage. Perhaps most importantly, there is the tinsel hanging at the back of the stage. There are many mysteries to be read in the sparkling of the tinsel. Much information is suspected to be encoded there. In the kinks of the individual strands of the tinsel, *in the way the shimmer moves up and down the strands, when the spotlight shines, and when it does not. Much may be read in the language of tinsel, and Goerges is the preeminent living expert.*

What does Goerges read in the tinsel? My dear readers, and if I may be so bold, my friends, brace yourselves: it is written in the tinsel that when next the spotlight comes on the entity will arrive, and that those waiting on the turret to observe the vista will indeed observe the final battle that determines whether Sickleburg survives or joins the atlas of the lost, the ruined, and the forgotten cities of history. HS.

The air is too hot for this time of year, it feels like the whole world has a fever. In the plaza in central Sickleburg, the sign over the storefront now reads: "Herkimer's Polymer Showroom." We thought the place was exclusive before but it's even harder to get inside now. When people who can pay the cover charge go through the door we get a tiny glimpse of holograms of him, dancing, writhing, standing on pedestals. It's weird, a little, it's just odd, we think, that none of us can afford the charge to go in there. Something else is sick in this world, it's like another fever, a fever of money. It's all flowed and clotted in too few bank accounts.

Afternoon is just translating into evening when a new vent opens. The New Synth blaring from it punishingly loud. The news spreads like a ghostly influenza, dozens of us put in our earplugs, cluster around the vent for a chance to see our Polymer. Prepared for more than that.

There are too many vents, vents too ephemeral, for them all to have real names. We're calling this one the Hermand 12 Vent after the man who discovered it. Though giving someone credit for discovering this gaping hole in middle of a drought-blasted park, a blue lesion in the dead grass, trees leaning down into it where their roots are undermined, seems almost as strange as letting an explorer name a mountain.

Yes, this is the twelfth vent found by Hermand. We know it can't be just chance he keeps happening upon them. Maybe Hermand has an intuitive understanding of the cracks that indicate a vent will open soon. We think that all the synths have worn him a little too thin. No, not too thin, we all wish we could be that refined. A constant wide-eyed, ah, not exactly terror, inhabits him, it must be ecstasy instead. The pupils of his eyes are a dim shining red now like he's lit from within by some unknown energy.

Hermand is giving a soliloquy, It is heard, in the notes, in the chords, in the arpeggio, the song of what comes next, after the AMEN, it is why I am not afraid and why you should not be afraid either, we will be taken apart, but afterwards, put together more cleverly than before...

Our attention snatched away from Hermand as he paces up and down the length of the vent: Polymer is there. A woman spots him, There! Down at the base of the crack, dozens of yards down where boulders and dirt have sheared away. Tiny, his white jumpsuit dull before a seething green mist. He's haloed all around with coils of synth.

We came prepared this time. We're heavily armed. Swords, those of us who can afford them, pitchforks, shovels, hoes, rakes, poles with kitchen knives wired to the tips, clubs made of broken table legs. Polymer reaches up to us, we scream, pour down the crooked path.

Polymer lets us reach him, stretches out his hands to us. His face is a perfect blank but his back is arched, his limbs contorted with emotion. If we are drawing power from him then he is drawing many times more power from us. We don't mind, so brightly is he burning, must burn to succeed down here, that power must have some supply.

He moves through us like we're a shallow puddle. Touches the synthpad, his fingers now strong and sure, fizzing tendrils of synth stab down and like the mandibles of an ant start carving the soil into a staircase.

Hermand's voice is still audible as we descend, though the echoes chop and glitch away the words themselves. We are encased in dread and doom, but at least we're armed. We know that "armed" is generous. It's just that it is so much harder to meet your fate empty-handed, you never know what to do with your fingers.

The stairway cuts through funerary cysts. Mummies bisected, showing all their layers, like in a museum. The green mist shredded by our descent fills in behind us. It smells faintly of beef broth.

With a last stroke of the synths the ceiling and wall crumble away. A wide room is revealed, an occult laboratory, filled with metal racks for test tubes and etched skulls. Dried crocodilians, circuit boards in ranks blasted by oscillating fans. Low, flickering light. We line up along the edge of the room, watch Polymer stride towards the center. There are hints of presence around the edges, the darkness there is thick with motionless withrons in clear suits. The swirling of New Synth has damped down, itching in our minds like a louse that has somehow slipped under the skin.

Just before Polymer reaches the center of the lab, a switch booms, and a vast column of white light appears. Lord Abisma stands at a small, battered table covered with yellow notepads. With one hand he is writing down some notes, his concave face bent toward them. In the other, he holds Polymer's old rapier. Tip on the floor, his hand on the hilt.

Standing behind Abisma, their hands behind their backs, heads bent down, are Captain Edgmond, Mauve, and Hictor. We grip our weapons more tightly. To many of us this feels like a terrible trap, but there is nowhere else we want to be. If Polymer is to meet his doom here, then we will as well.

Lord Abisma finishes his writing, turns to Polymer.

"Oh, there you are. I knew it couldn't be long before you showed up."

Polymer doesn't answer, takes several steps forwards. He touches the synthpad, causing four smoking spines to probe out before him. Abisma glances at them, then at us.

"An audience!" Back to Polymer. He places the rapier on the table with notepads. "Excuse me for just a moment..."

He steps over to the three hunters, lifts Hictor by grabbing the fabric of his doublet under his chin. He turns so that we and Polymer can see what happens next. He lifts Hictor's face to his own hollow skull, a motion slow and horribly intimate, like someone performing an unfamiliar sex act by following carefully written instructions.

Hictor's face fits inside Abisma's. Abisma's hand floats up and with it he massages the back of Hictor's head. Hictor's head half-swallowed. The hunter's limbs flail and tense, curling up like twisted straw papers touched by a drop of water. Abisma jerks orgasmically. Inside of a minute, he is holding a shriveled skin that dangles inside

Hictor's clothing. He tosses the skin without concern for where it might fall and a tiny withron in a small, kettle-like armor skitters over to catch it.

Polymer moves his hand and the synthspines around him begin to rotate. A tall, thin man cries out, What are you waiting for, go get him, Polymer!

Abisma looks at us with a smile that's hard to read because of his unique physiology. His features seemed bloated. "If you don't mind waiting just one minute more," he says, and lifts Mauve by the wrappings under her throat.

We are muttering amongst ourselves, most of us can see that the problem is not quite so easily solved as we might wish. Polymer can't just rush Abisma, he's too far away, before he can charge he must first come within a distance that allows him some chance at a definitive strike. He takes several more steps forward, the synths whirling now like the blades of a blender. We do the only thing we can, we boo Abisma.

Abisma cocks his head at us, distracted for just a moment. Mauve's right arm, which had seemed to be constrained by her wrists being bound behind her back, windmills around, her hand bearing a small knife. She swings it sideways at Abisma's head. He bends his neck, we didn't know that creatures other than lizards could move like that, the movement so sharp and sudden we should have heard something snap, and Mauve's blade slides through the nothingness that would be the bridge of his nose were his face not inside out. She has already dropped the knife as a lost cause, and now her leg is moving, bending around weirdly as in a difficult dance. Her foot connects with Abisma's ribcage, a hollow thud, like she's kicked a metal barrel.

A flash of shock in his sunken eyes. Abisma clenches his fist where he holds Mauve and she screams. Then he straightens his arm to fling her away, into the darkness at the back of the lab, where gleaming withrons clink together in their zeal to crush her.

Polymer has taken another four steps forward. Just a few more now and he might be able to catch Abisma with a lunge. We're clenching our own fists so hard that our knuckles turn white, blood drips down from our palms to our wrists. Our teeth are gritted tight as mortar and pestle. Polymer's blades of synth open, like the blades of a fractal jackknife, he needs just a few feet more.

Abisma rapidly strides back out of Polymer's range, to Captain Edgmond's side. We groan in frustration. Abisma steps behind Edgmond, and now we notice that something is strange about this hunter's appearance, his head, drooped onto his chest, is entirely cocooned in pinkish fibers. Abisma leans out from behind Edgmond's back and we all see that he has just untied the hunter's hands.

"Since your audience is so eager to see you fight, I'll let you make the difficult decision of how to deal with poor Captain Edgmond," Abisma says, retreating further in the gloom of the lab, out of the light. "You should know that his actions are not entirely his own right now, though theoretically many of his thoughts and much of personality remains. If there were any way to clean the silk off his face he might even recover from the brain damage."

Abisma's hand, all that's left of him within the sharp pillar of light, snaps its fingers. The white light turns wine-red, our eyes are confused, it takes us a moment to make sense of what we're seeing, there is a reddish blur in the air over Captain Edgmond, it comes into focus if we stare not directly at it but just to the side, a towering blur twice his height, it gives the impression of limbs and nerves, an upside-down insect's body, a twelve-foot tall ruddy see-through louse balanced with its pulsing proboscis on Edgmond's head.

Edgmond moves suddenly, his head still slumped down, he scoops up the clear rapier from where Abisma left it, walks briskly towards Polymer like he's slightly late to catch his train. And the red louse moves with him, it seems to have no weight of its own, dangling through a crack from another world. Its gauzy spinnerets move about Edgmond's face like it's massaging his aura. Abisma's laughter echoes from the darkness.

A woman exhales a long breath and whispers, Kill him already... We all feel the same way, even those of us who used to love Edgmond. He's gone corrupt. He has to die. What the fuck? Our blood is up. A bleeping drumbeat rattles our skulls. A clanking clatter like a hill of cowbells. Give us just a nudge and we'll be spilling down there to slaughter Edgmond ourselves.

Polymer adjusts the synths, tapping on the synthpad like he's entering some familiar PIN, the fan of blades all swing together, blossom closing for the night, a multiblade unsolid sword congealed around his right arm, it starts at the elbow, comes to a conical point a yard past the end of his fingertips. Wisps of smoke rise along its length, and a foul chemical smell, wherever the blade passes, the air is burnt.

Haunted Edgmond moves toward Polymer, his path a constricting spiral. The rapier down at his side, clutched loosely, as if he's forgotten about it. Polymer walking slowly but without pause, straight for

Edgmond. There should be some type of calculus that will tell us when the two must clash.

The rapier thrusts, the synthblade bats it aside. They've met! The synthblade chops downward, the slender rapier barely nudges it aside. Then the rapier tilts, stabs forward, already in position, slides screaming down the last length of the insubstantial synthblade, a hole appears in Polymer's jumpsuit. A crown of blood appears around the hole.

Polymer fights with elbow, knee, synthblade only tertiary, his plastic face shining with a fine mist of artificial sweat. Edgmond must keep angling backward, he needs a certain minimum distance between them before impalement becomes feasible. The two blades bat at one another experimentally. A hush is over us, we cannot expend an iota of energy except for watching the fight, because we know that a match between two swords, even occult swords comprised of synths, can be decided by a single blow.

Polymer steps forward and to the right, swings sideways to the left at Edgmond's midsection. Edgmond deflects, ripostes brilliantly and we all discover together that the rapier is now sticking into Polymer's left shoulder, through the joint, a foot of the clear blade, smeared with blood, is visible sticking out of his back. The blood rushes from our faces like we're the ones just stabbed. Polymer takes the last second he has, pulls himself closer to Edgmond, and thrusts his blade of synth upward into the shining red louse attached to Edgmond's head.

Pink threads explode outward, the air shivers like the grinding of fractured bone. With the fingers of his impaled arm he touches his synthpad and the petals of his sword unfurl, they snick outward, a rat king made of switchblades, and the louse is cut into six wedge-shaped pieces which drift sideways, drizzling little clots of white jelly segments like the fragments of a tapeworm.

The two hunters collapse together. Edgmond spasming, clearly dying, Polymer still strong enough to probe at the rapier now standing straight up out of his shoulder joint, though not strong enough to pull it free. We are too emotional to clap. There is some broken weeping, some freely flowing tears.

The light switches back to white from red, and suddenly we are able to see the spatter of blood over the two combatants, red tracked around the arena, glistening wedges left by Polymer's running shoes, ovals and squares from Edgmond's boots. You can read the map of the whole fight there. Maybe. We can't. Tears in our eyes, and we don't have the expertise anyway. We're no hunters, just citizens.

Lord Abisma walks back into the light. New Synth rises like miasmic seepage from a field of pillaged graves. Unhurried, it still takes no time for him to reach Polymer and Edgmond. Edgmond he ignores, already dead. The hacked louse drifts in pieces in the darkness above us. Thin strands of glistening ichor drip from the pieces, hang down between them in bows.

Abisma crouches over Polymer. He lifts our hero's head in his hands, Polymer's neck extends, his body dangling downward like a doll. His face disappears into the bowl of Abisma's.

We are shocked once again into silence. Polymer's right hand twitches. Abisma's body jerks like he's accidentally fallen asleep, then he lets Polymer down.

Abisma stares down at Polymer, then over at us. "Fucking hell. His face."

Polymer, lying sprawled on his back, his right hand flies up, grips the rapier sticking into his shoulder by its blade, flips the blade, and plunges it into Abisma's side.

Abisma roars, clasps his hands together and smashes them down at Polymer like a hammer but Polymer rolls onto his stomach, awkwardly, and Abisma misses. Polymer flops again, onto his back. Somehow still holding onto the rapier. He touches the synthpad, and a slit opens in the floor just beyond him. He manages one more roll, drops into the slit, and is gone from sight.

Abisma stands, crosses his arms, stands over the slit and peers down into it. He turns to us with some finality, some kind of inverted smirk on his wrongly perfect face.

"Don't worry, I'll catch him later. For now I'll be happy to make you suffer for his behavior." He ignores the wound at his waist. Gaping bloodless behind the slit in his silk shirt.

There is no escape for any of us now, unlike the last time we me Abisma. Any veterans of that encounter here now? Yes, a few, and this time we clutch our rickety weapons, we clutch for our courage where it seems to be slipping, seeping away. Abisma flickers to us, lays about with his fists, which strike us with the force of twenty-pound sledgehammers. No time for bruises to form, his fists rupture flesh, break bone, burst organs. We try to deflect the blows, but he's moving fast, jerking like a tape reel run at the wrong speed, fast-forwarding to get to the good parts, he knocks a man's head sideways so hard the skull deflates like a kickball, neck folding over like a wilted lily, he punches a woman so hard in the stomach her spine breaks, he clubs someone in the shoulder so hard it looks like their arm is attached to the bottom of their ribcage, though it's not really attached to anything any more.

Yet we are crushed so tight around him that some of our wild blows land accidentally. The stopped clock hand occasionally hitting the right time. His shirt is in tatters, wounds growing on his pallid flesh underneath it. In the manner of a romance novel cover model, he looks more and more unstoppable the more damage to shirt and self he accumulates. Under the flesh is a hard rind, something dark and varnished. A hoe bites into his clay-like muscle, reveals black bones of petrified wood.

We've made him angry enough that he unclenches his fists. His fingers like claws grip a body in two places, rip it open, he flings the two halves aside, blood and entrails arcing like comet tails. He twists limbs, instant spiral fracture, he reaches through a back, fingers pinched into a beak, grabs a face, pulls one of us through another's body.

A crowd of withron surgeons has gathered, pressed rapt against the inner surfaces of their hunched glass armor, with its long and many jointed arms braced against the floor. It's not easy for an audience to adjust to being the show. Abisma has just lifted one of us and folded him like a sweater, a great crackling of bone and popping of organs, and it takes those of us who are still alive a moment to make sense of what we are seeing, that we just witnessed Abisma destroy seventy people in the space of two minutes.

The only reason we're still living is that before Abisma reached the others we ran to the slit in the floor down which Polymer escaped. And there's only one slight chance we have now of surviving. Thirty of us, into the hole.

There's no clever synth-cut staircase here, just a series of steep ledges alternating to the left and right, carved in desperation. It's partly a leap, partly a fall, with which we follow Polymer away from the blood-spattered laboratory. There are a bare dozen of us, we've dropped our weapons, our chests sting from where we have fallen too quickly. The thunder of New Synth is omnipresent, our brains have grown accustomed, and we are starting to hear the subtleties in the structure of it, the sine waves like serrated scalpels, the clicks of compressed song, whole symphonies encoded in a single bleep. This time we won't let Polymer escape from us, we will finally know where he goes when he ventures beyond the Castle that floats like a parasite beyond Sickleburg.

We run out of ledges, fall finally. Float downward. The sky above us is an infinitely broad, bumpy plain of blue stone. Scrawled with clear sigils. We land on a field of black-bladed grass that grows from powdery white soil. Seed pods rustle around us like tiny rattles. There is no way to reach the black slit in blue stone leading back above, it's horribly clear. Even a human pyramid or, more wobbly, a human ladder, wouldn't suffice. For some reason we start to laugh. It hardly matters now, we just have to find Polymer.

A woman cries out, There he is!

His white jumpsuit stands out against the black grass. He keeps looking back to us, there is nothing to read of course in the expression of his face, something in his posture, it almost makes us regret our decision to follow him, even knowing that had we remained above Abisma would have torn us into gobbets. He keeps gesturing back to the slit. How can he really expect us to leave him now, even if it were possible to reach.

Polymer's voice floats to us over the rattling grass: "Behind you!"

We turn, see what has caused the rustling, in the absence of otherworldly wind, creeping up on us through the tall grass, short figures no higher than our navels, their heads swollen and squared around the edges, cube-heads, covered with curly hair of various colors. Their eyes spin hypnotically, freezing us as if our veins have been filled with plastic resin, in the first instant, but then we forget our troubles.

A few of us, at the margin of the group, closer to Polymer, run as these cube-headed folk begin leisurely to eat our comrades, small neat nibbles of flesh drooling blood, the eyes spin, polite squeaky voices direct limbs to be lowered, the better to be reached. We lie down. We're in an orgy of tiny mouths, red pearl teeth. One last erotic tug at the flesh and then we'll let our eyelids fall, energy spent.

Just a handful of us left to follow Polymer into the hinterland. We look back and forth to one another as we run trying not to stumble. Wonder which one is going to be the last left standing.

The ground drops away, black grass down an endless slope. There, great swampy New Synth organs rumble. We recognize the lie in that NEW, there's nothing novel about this synth. It seeped through to the Castle just as the Castle's music seeped through to Sickleburg. If this blue abyss is the ultimate source of the synths then they have nothing to do with our aboveground lives. Except in their capacity to destroy us.

Polymer has run far ahead. A blurred landscape stretches before us. This multibranching vale, dropping in ribbed chasms, pulsing with magenta radiation, we can see for millions of miles. Mountains, or are they beasts, come together with glacial steps, bounce, dance, merge together like puzzles snapping to.

A thing like a walking palm tree crossed with ten radially-fused parrots, taller than a hundred skyscrapers, a thing like a shelf of burning stone rising higher than a tidal wave, swaying like a tapestry woven of a billion fiery cobras, a thing like an eyeball with an eyeball inside it with another eyeball inside it, and an eyeball outside it, eyeballs all the way up and all the way down, floating like some mad moon, seemingly built of a substance like amethyst jelly one moment, like hard crystal the next, like a flickering mist the next. One last shriek, Polymer, wait for us! We're right behind you!

The black grass is tall. We can't see Polymer any more. He has outpaced us, dashing on deep into the primordial synthooze. Tendrils loop around our limbs. Like tiny tongues press into the pupils our eyes. Fruiting pods swell in our ears. Bodies striped with abrasions from the blades. As we die we hang suspended and beads of our blood turn pink then brown in the white dirt.

Those of us still up in Sickleburg wonder at the tremors that shake the streets, topple the shoddier buildings. The air has a burnt smell to it. Usually that means something is about to malfunction. That something already has malfunctioned but we just haven't figured out what, yet. We'll know soon enough, when it explodes.

As we wait, gathered in the plazas and alleys, a late edition of our favorite tabloid comes out. Ink like the fluid from the gills of rotting mushrooms smears our fingers and foreheads.

Dear readers, you may be certain that your faithful correspondent is as eager as any to learn what is happening to our hero Polymer at this moment, which is why I took it upon myself to extrovert my astral self through the prism of my crystal ball, and so steal into the depths of the synthcrack and report back to you firsthand what I saw therebelow.

I descended quickly along the course blazed by Polymer, through the remains of a massacre in a hidden laboratory, the limbs and viscera stained black, crawling all over with winking electronic maggots. I forced myself through a narrow slit, down a series of switchbacks, into that azure hellscape beyond the Castle. I flashed past a carnival of carnivorous carnality, passed the ones who escaped being eaten only to find themselves dangling dead, knotted in loops and whorls of black grass. I drifted down a long valley, at the bottom of which I saw the white-suited speck of Polymer, his arms raised in ecstatic welcome. Lest you gather the opposite impression of what I mean to say, he was not facing me; he was not welcoming this intangible sylph. It was three impossibly vast phantasms he greeted. They bore down on him, their attention shimmering at him in rippling cones.

Naturally I forge ahead. I come to Polymer, where he labors over a shining altar in the shape of an inverted pyramid. His hand moves over the synthpad. His rapier lies on the altar. Worms of light wriggle through his flesh. His neoprene face warped with the strain of the skinless flesh behind it. The synth is solid here. Great humming bricks of it. If I had a body, I suspect that I could not breathe.

Polymer sees me! I bob my body, in lieu of a bow. He gestures desperately, globes of staticky cyan synth forming around his joints. I will come back to him; more intriguing in that moment are the three mountainous shapes just beyond the altar whose cones of attention now touch and probe at me. These three, so powerful that the great Shhoggafrog is but their puniest tadpole. There is a shivering in my brain like the last clenching twitch before orgasm becomes inevitable.

I am greeted by KLRTH whose trunk is girdled with tentacles blizzarding spores, part vegetable part infinite parrot, hooks like mouthparts of a cosmic parasite sink into my astral non-flesh, draw me closer, my astral non-face bending like there is a metal bar in the shape of a smile between my lips, KLRTH blasts steam like a ring of volcanoes, I drift up into that crystal embrace, steam like acid scouring away all my imperfections, but by then I have drifted somehow into the zone of ZRWLDR, stern icy scales rising, of course the earth is flat, I can see how it stretches infinitely to heaven and hell, this close to it there's *nothing else that I can see, im sucked in by its unstoppable beams, the earth is nothing but ZRWLDR, swirling pulsing ripples, covered with something like a thick furry pelt, like fuzzy flames burning clear, pink, yellow, pale green, oh stars, i am witnessed at this juncture by HNDLB, hello imust be going, iam seen through like the wet sheet, like the onion skin, like the ghost i am, seen through by an eye seeing through an eye seeing through itself, seen through by another, HNDLB sees every atom of me, knows that inside the atoms are quarks, inside the quarks are ilths, inside the ilths are groogs, inside the groogs are whole universes vibrating in tune with the song of HNDLB's command, if they fight over me another moment I will be shorn into three lobes, but what's this, beyond these three i must push ahead, because i can see now that beyond these three there is another, god, two infinite walls meet in an infinite corner, a corner known as QZRM, god, there is no god, there is no god but QZRM [sic]*

[Note: These scribblings were found in the office of popular staff writer Homer Spline, and since we know that all of you are as eager as any of us to learn what is happening to our hero Polymer, it was decided to print them without alteration. However, suffice it to say that Spline is no longer employed here at the Sickleburg Gaze. We would have fired him immediately even if his twitching corpse were not found along with these chickenscratch paperbabblings, his skull caved in and seemingly containing nothing but a wisps of a whitish substance like cotton candy, beside a cracked and smoking crystal ball. We do not condone such occult sources, however sensational the intelligence they produce. Keep those opinion letters coming! We can't wait to hear your take on this breaking story. Ed.]

Sickleburg is shaking on its foundations now. The air is shuddering, like the heat that rises from banked embers. Except it's cold, the streets so cold. The frost forms on the glass in concentric patterns. The bellowing of the synths shaking into those patterns. We are in denial, watching our Polymer sex tapes like they are barrels full of burning trash, desperate for a bit of warmth, tainted as it might be. All the potatoes left in the bins are mutated into the faces of hideous goblins, and they taste like wood pulp. We are starving, at last. We might be lucky enough to slip into comas from lack of food before the city subsides sideways into oblivion. Come back to us, Polymer. Without you we are pathetic.

Life on the Watchers' turret maintains some level of normality. We have been accepted into the sect. We share in the cooking duties, and the cleaning duties. To be honest we do more than the others, not that this is unfair, is the universal way of the new arrival. There are many techniques for cooking pigeon and rat over a burn barrel. It is difficult but not impossible to grill a pizza. Our potatoes are thin and bad but at least require fewer slices before they are ready to toast on long, stiff wires, one frenchfry at a time.

Of course we hear the chaos coming from the streets of Sickleburg, of course we wonder how our old fellows will survive the doom that is sure to come to those streets. We are the chosen ones now, there is an excitement at first barely contained, then not contained at all, it is said that the tinsel has spoken, that all this tension will soon break.

They must have heard something, because the people of Sickleburg are gathered around our turret. There's an abandoned building across the street, a bank, we think, and the roof is full of tents and sleeping bags. They keep planks at the edges, they're waiting for us to give the signal letting them lay the planks and cross over, when the time is right. Across the perpendicular street, an empty school, the even wider roof is home to a mob, they are trying to building an arching bridge to our turret. But without us building back they'll never make it to the keystone before the whole thing collapses to the cobblestones below.

Agat Estoc preaches day and night, her face turned into a haggard mask, her eyes blazing marbles reflecting the light of our long awaited glory. Ether sharpens her sword while listening to her mother's sermons. It's sharp enough now to cut concrete, at least with the first blow. Father Zeero in his masked masks shares plans with us that give us guidance for what to do in case of certain other things happening. We'll share soon enough what these plans are, or it will become obvious, when we start to perform one of them.

Goerges' voice comes from the holy parapet: The tinsel is speaking! The time is up! The Great Show is about to begin!

What perfect timing, those of us who just joined the watchers, we all cram onto the ledge, and see the tinsel shining in the margin of the spotlight, which still illuminates a blank stage. The world itself pulling back like stage curtains as they are drawn open, the aperture onto the stage widens. The Estocs, the other watchers, we the neophytes, all gasp together, as we understand that what lets us see the stage is a vent like any other. Just like all of them across Sickleburg. The stage is in the Castle.

In from stage right walks Polymer. We are struck by a hush, then burst with fiery applause. Polymer looks to us, across a distance of many blocks, and bows his head. His posture is perfect, his white jumpsuit blazing like a comet, torn in many places but sewn together with vibrating blue light that branches like the veins in marble. His slicked hair scraped flat and to the side. His face blank and still as that of a caryatid who holds up the world. His old clear rapier hangs at his waist. He swivels his feet, turning from us, facing center stage and beyond it, stage left.

In from the darkness of stage left, where the ridge of reality is curled and thickened by synths, walks Lord Abisma. We hiss and flick our fingers at him, disdainful gestures as if to dislodge a bug. He turns to us, performs briefly a hieratic gesture, arms raised, elbows crooked, hands clawed just so. He has no weapon that we can see.

The two of them stand there, on opposite sides of the small stage, and Sickleburg holds its breath. We have the best view, and we are being watched through telescope and binoculars from the buildings behind us. The ones watching us know what we are watching, it is as though they are watching second hand. Sometimes watching someone watch something is almost as good as seeing it yourself. They watch us, frozen with anticipation, and they are too.

A drone of synths weighty as the flight of bumblebees fills the stage, drifts to the turret, drifts to the streets where we crowd as close as we can, hoping to find some way to see what's happening, as it is almost physically painful to us that there we can't see what happening, we just have to watch people who are watching those who see what is happening. At least we can hear the synths. And the roar that erupts when the two combatants finally come together in a windmilling of limbs.

Abisma swings his arms like smiting rods. He doesn't care if he'll get hit once or twice with Polymer's blade. Polymer is patient, backing away in a large circle. When he is given the opportunity he darts his rapier towards Abisma like the tongue of a snake who's just tasting the air.

Look who it is, here on the roof of the abandoned school with us, it's Herkimer! The first anyone has seen her for weeks. She is wearing lemon-yellow wraparound sunglasses, her hair shoots up from her scalp like a black tornado.

From the abandoned bank we watch the people on the abandoned school crowd around Herkimer. They grasp at the hems of her collarless jacket like the threads are infused with Polymer's cool. Planks drop into place, and we merge with the other group.

Polymer slides around the stage with eerie movements, each seems impossible in the moment that he's doing it, how can a human being flex and bend in such a way, seems inevitable in the moment after he's done it. The rapier balanced in his hand like a weightless wand. Abisma rage-hops around the stage like a humanoid flea. His gelled curls whip around his concave face. The blows of his arms, any of which could fold Polymer in half, except that Polymer manages to bend himself out of danger just in time.

Lord Abisma's voice fills the gaps between the buildings. Sounds both faint and booming. It's as though the voice is coming from some unknown distance behind him, this otherworldly drone, and Abisma's just a mouthpiece, a tin can tied to the end of a string:

"A clap is coming, you worm, all of you worms, a great clap, have you ever considered being crushed thin as a sheet of paper by your own applause, ha, that's right, you vermin, you intolerable pest, soon you'll know, you'll be flat as woven silk, you flatworm, I can see that you don't know yet what I mean, but soon you shall, if by any chance you manage to defeat me then you will quickly learn what I mean, be flattened like a pancake, and all of your wormy friends, in your paper city, in your false world, nothing but squiggles of ink, flat as paper..." The drone rises and falls like a prayer.

Herkimer tells us of the blank shell at the heart of Polymer's personality. It's what you first encounter, when you start to get to know him. Underneath the blank shell is a thin rind of frightening, amoral bitterness. But this is false as well. Underneath the rind, which is just part of his hunter's survival mechanism, is the warm true center of his personality. It's hidden under all these shells and skins and layers, that's all. So worth knowing. A man sidles up, whispers, What do you have to sell us, Herkimer? She shrugs. "Nothing, not any more."

Polymer is slowing down, slightly, while Abisma is moving faster than before. Leaving some sort of blurred trails behind himself as he lurches across the stage. His hands outstretched like a ghoul trying to catch rattling fleeing bones. He must have some secret technique for adjusting his own momentum. Like he's attached to hundreds of differently-aligned pendulums, can choose on which one to pivot, swing a different direction at any particular moment. Polymer parries each strike with less and less vigor. Each time he avoids getting smashed, the hope that he'll forever manage to keep avoiding getting smashed seems less viable.

Ether Estoc is staring intently across the open air that separates us from the view, as if by the force of her gaze she could bridge that gap. Her sword in her hand, she wants nothing more than to join the battle. Her brother is falling back under Abisma's piledriver fists. That perfect concave face is twisted into a bestial grimace, the silk shirt shredded with rapier blows that didn't quite connect. Ether's teeth are gritted hard enough that we hear the grinding.

Polymer pauses, bats away Abisma's arm, though it drives him to one knee. He taps his synthpad, he's prepared for this. All across the turret and the surrounding buildings, a whooshing intake of breath. The rapier glows bright white for a moment, a crystal in the light of the sun, and Polymer stabs Abisma through the knee.

Abisma shrieks a laugh, he staggers. Socks Polymer in the side, we can hear the sick crack of ribs. The squelch of organs. Polymer twists the rapier, stuck halfway through the kneecap, it sprouts gleaming synthorns, and when Abisma surges up from the stage's board, he leaves his leg behind. Oooooooooo. We think we're cheering. Abisma looks down, in shock, wavering on one leg, and we have to say that we're in a bit of our own shock.

He crouches on the leg, lifts Polymer up, and with exquisite balance, holding Polymer upside down by his ankles, tears him in half from the groin to the sternum. Fuck. So he wasn't so much in shock as we thought. As we hoped.

Countless blue worms hold Polymer together. Cyan

sparks dance along a second skeleton he maintains inside himself now. Abisma pulls the legs apart, farther, farther, but his vast strength has met its limit, and the ruptured hips snap back together, Polymer is spinning around, a pinwheel, Abisma fights to hold on, leaning back as if from a slashing propeller.

When Polymer is fully upright, he presses himself closer into Abisma's grip. Abisma struggles to drop the hunter but now it's too late. Like a soaking unwelcome embrace, he can't escape. Polymer drops his sword, grabs the hair at the sides of Abisma's head, laces his fingers through it. He worms himself closer, presses his face into the hollow of Abisma's. Abisma hopping backwards, his single leg flexing like a pneumatic piston gone wild.

Tears in Herkimer's eyes. Zeero and Agat Estoc, their hands clasped at their chests, Goerges reads Lord Abisma's epitaph from the wall of tinsel. He died as he was born, from the cauldron of New Synth.

A synthcorona forms around Polymer's plastic face. Hail to the crown. Razor horns penetrate Abisma's inward-curving flesh. The horns merge, and segments of Abisma's head fall sideways, separated like the parts of some conveniently evolved fruit. No space for a brain in that hollow head, just thick mats of wriggling synthworms, puce and chartreuse, seeping a pattern of paisley static.

The hollow body falls back, limbs all bent and splayed like a corpse that has hit the sidewalk after falling from a high building. Polymer stands, pulsing with threads of blue glitter. All that's keeping him together. We lose our minds to some extent.

Polymer raises his rapier to us. We clap hard enough

to cause bruising and later, swelling. Our voices rush out of our mouths in rasping cheers. One hand pressing into his synthpad, Polymer points with his sword and where he points, branching synthbolts fry the air into flying bridges.

First the turret of the holy view is connected, and we surge across, the Estocs, old Goerges, the rest of us initiates. Lightning strikes again and again, cannonfire in the distance lagging behind its lightspeed, and synthbridges connect the turret to the abandoned bank, to the abandoned school. We surge across. The citizens of Sickleburg rise, we help one another across the splintery, shivering bridges, we swarm the tiny stage. Our hands outstretched, to bask in the blue glow of glory coming off Polymer something like sweat, something like a pheromone, we are in the presence of majesty, and if we're not, then we are crushing forward to get there. As we press forward we are filled in from behind, streets climbing the ladder, advancing over the bridges like the fingers of a giant hand made of synth, splayed over the stage. Polymer's rapier raised, a bar of hope.

He lowers the rapier. "Friends—" We shout over him, doesn't matter what he's trying to say to us because our feelings, in our hundreds, are more intense than his could possibly be, our voices combine, rattling bricks, vibrating the air. The tinsel still shivering on the back wall, dancing flashes of light up and down, Goerges alone looking past Polymer, saying, Oh...

Abisma's body is jerked into the air like a toy on a string. A vertical line like a fold in a piece of paper bisects his broken form. He lacks a third dimension, is folding in over himself. Behind the stage the tinsel all blows out, the bricks tumble away, revealing lightyears of nothingness sprinkled with cosmic dust.

Brown stars, smearing radioactive light across the infinite abyss. Abisma floats backwards, the vestiges of his body drooping like rags, his left side, an infinite wall, his right side, an infinite wall. Where they meet, the infinite corner, as high as the universe. Goerges reads in the tinsel, QZRM, before he suffers a stroke, falls drooling to the floor, we trample him underfoot, shuffling ecstatically.

Polymer turns. He beckons to us, and we follow. Leaping up over the rim of the stage, Ether Estoc is the first to reach him, swinging her massive sword over her head, her fried vocal battle cry buzzing in our ears. They run toward the corner, QZRM, we rush behind them. Zeero Estoc, removed his mask, his face is like featureless dough beneath it. It's what happens when you wear a mask for too many years. His faintest smile. Agat Estoc, whispering pointless spells. Ready to punch a wall if it would help save Sickleburg. Herkimer, tears streaming down her face, forcing her way through the mob to stand at Polymer's side.

The great corner, Abisma-rags now fluttering like pennants a hundred yards up, the walls like planes of smoky quartz. A rich hum comes off them, Polymer and the Estocs stop, their heads bent together as they formulate a plan. We surge past them, and melt in the impossible humming. Flesh drips down, blood fizzles away, a brothy red mist rises up to the knees of those who come after, bones standing for a second as the veins are whipped away, in a snarl, some magic trick. We laugh. The walls of the corner are coming together. What happens when they meet? The corner QZRM will compress the entirety of our world into a wafer. When the walls meet there will be nothing.

Polymer touches his synthpad, scaffolds of synthlines rise up, pressing in to the shuddering quartz. High overhead the dripping shreds of Lord Abisma flutter mockingly. We climb in, under, around the scaffolds, as the quartz walls press closer the scaffolds jump and warp, we are pinched into pieces. Limbs folded off, spindle and mutilate, a rich stew of blood and tears, Polymer tapping at something like a gleaming insubstantial console that has emerged from his chest. Buttresses fly up, bridges arc from wall to wall, guy lines strain, to keep the world from being closed.

Our efforts are making a glorious music. If nothing else can be said of them, this triumph, this final triumph, we share it with Polymer. Our hearts exploding, this is how generous he is, he shares this last gift with us. The bass thunders, marrow boils. The scaffolds dance, buckle, synthsplinters flying through us. But there are always more of us to come from behind, the whole population of Sickleburg, drawn to this spot, still surging in over the bridges.

Ether and Agat, back to back, at the pit of the corner, pressing into the opposing walls with their hands and legs, Zeero crouched down, back to the corner itself, limbs spread wide. The quartz walls groan closer, the Estocs shriek. Polymer plays his fingers over the synthkeys, spars shooting out, through us, exploding ribs, shuddering skulls, dazzles of light playing on the slowly constricting limits of our world.

Polymer in that moment, his head bowed in perfect concentration. There is a kind of peace there, the way his arms move shows no strain of effort, his back arched with the type of concentration that cannot be broken by pain or calamity. His jumpsuit is black with blood. His blue face spiraled with gory smears. We don't regret a thing. We stand on a thick mulch of shattered bones, liquified flesh, congealed blood, sizzling fragments of synth like radioactive embers, and we cannot honestly say that we regret a thing. We love you, Polymer.

The scaffolds are popping, breaking. Zeero disappears into the apex of the corner. Ether and Agat, crushed. Ether's sword raised is that last thing we see of her. Spars and buttresses crumbling. The corner has closed to forty-five degrees. Polymer's frantic fingers slow, we're in the coda now. Behind us, Sickleburg, the buildings all empty now anyway, accordioned together, the streets bunching up, the plazas crumpling. How silly was it that we obsessed over potatoes. How silly, when this was all that was in store for us? To be honest, this is the best we could have hoped for. A glorious blaze. Who wants to fade out peacefully? The corner QZRM now has forty degrees. Synths sounding like human voices, no, more perfect than that, rise from Polymer, he is infused with them. The mulched Sickleburgers rise in a tide, flowing out from the corner, which has now thirty-five degrees. Synths snap. Polymer falls silent. None of us has the arms or hands left to clap now, all twisted into a mass. Thirty degrees. Polymer stands, he's still standing, somehow. Lines of synth around him like an exoskeleton. Beams poking into the closing quartz walls. He stands at the center of the storm, bonechips flooding up around his knees. Twenty-five degrees. All of Sickleburg is smashing together like the vanes of a folding fan. Twenty degrees. Polymer takes off the synthpad. A few of us still have the strength to gasp. We gasp. Fifteen degrees. QZRM seems for a moment to pause in its closing. Polymer stands naked of the synths. For a moment, it doesn't seem so strange that once he was one of us. No, it's still closing, ten degrees. Polymer speaks, "Thank you all. I mean that. Thanks for everything." Five degrees. Polymer bows. The corner closes, and the world is gone.

Caleb Wilson writes weird fiction and creates weird computer games like Cannonfire Concerto, Lime Ergot, Six Gray Rats Crawl Up The Pillow, and The Northnorth Passage. He lives in Illinois with his wife and works in a public library.

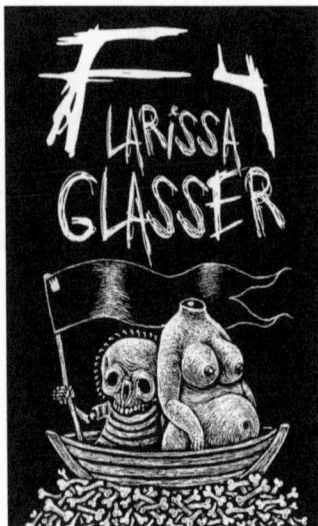

F4
Larissa Glasser

A cruise ship on the back of a sleeping kaiju. A transgender bartender trying to come terms with who she is. A rift in dimensions known as The Sway. A cruel captain. A storm of turmoil, insanity and magic is coming together and taking the ship deep into the unknown. What will Carol the bartender learn in this maddening non-place that changes bodies and minds alike into bizarre terrors? What is the sleeping monster who holds up the ship trying to tell her? What do Carol's fractured sense of self and a community of internet trolls have to do with the sudden pull of The Sway?

Polymer
Caleb Wilson

You've seen monster hunts before. You've watched as a guy with throwing axes and ninja stars ascends stairs to fight a big furry werewolf with tentacles or a floating head of indeterminate origin. You've seen hunters. But you've never seen Polymer. Polymer's got style, Polymer's got sex appeal, Polymer's got panache. And you, lucky reader, get to join us right behind the glass in Sickleburg Castle where the battle of the century is about to commence. Who is the man behind the music, the monsters, the guts, the gore and the glory? Get ready for an event like no other.

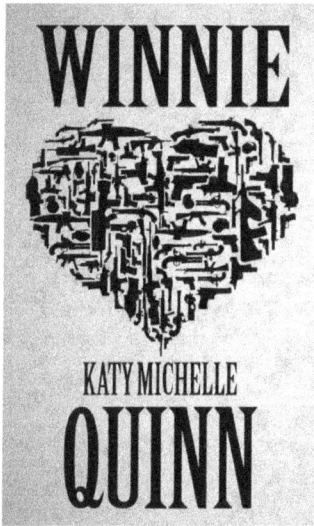

Winnie
Katy Michelle Quinn

Winnie and Colt forever. Winnie is Colt's one and only, Colt is Winnie's true love. Winnie is Colt's rifle. There is nothing Winnie wants more than to please Colt and since a rifle is everything the young cowboy's ever wanted, she certainly does that. But one day Winnie finds that she is not a rifle but in fact a woman. Can Winnie keep the sparks between them ignited, even if she isn't the gun of his dreams. What happens if she can't?

Eviscerator
Farah Rose Smith

Vex Valis—doctor. Vex Valis—rocker. Vex Valis—iconoclast. You would think Vex Valis has it all but what Vex has is a secret that rots away at her from her very core. Vex is infected with Gut Ghouls and will do anything to be rid of them, even if it means consorting with subterranean worms or blending science and the occult in dangerous and unsavory ways. You may envy Vex's jet setting Dark Wave scientist lifestyle but you won't when you see the trials incurred when she catches the attention of a being that rends people and worlds alike, the scrutiny of. . . The Eviscerator

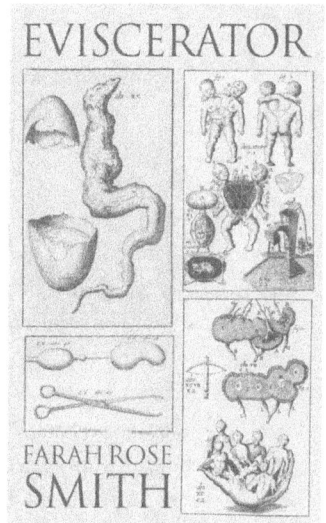

Fell Beauties
Leigham Shardlow

In the last outpost of ugliness in the world, beautiful people are falling from the sky. When Fat Janet is kicked out of the buffet where she has holed up for food and safety, she is forced to confront not only the reality of perfect falling bodies but the attentions of an overzealous plastic surgeon and his followers. She teams up with a mystery man in hopes of getting out of this alive but soon finds that confronting the problem head on is the only option. Can imperfection survive this beautiful disaster?

Crime of the Scene
Shawn Koch

A detective investigating a crime scene finds that nested inside this crime scene is another, and inside that another. Demons, physical deformity, body switching and endless trials await him as he begins to face his own transgressions. Reality grows distant as he soon comes to realize that he has stumbled not only upon the scene of many crimes but of all crimes. He might just have what it takes to get to the bottom of these but only if he gets to the bottom of himself.

CPSIA information can be obtained
at www.ICGtesting.com
Printed in the USA
BVHW03s1323250318
511475BV00001B/6/P

9 781621 052555